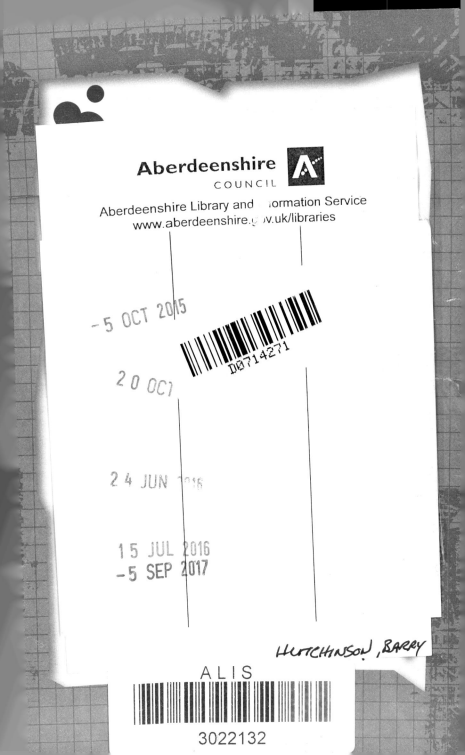

MEET THE CHARACTERS

Ben Tennyson
Always ready to go hero

Gwen Tennyson
Ben's cousin, with her
own superpowers

Kevin E. Levin
A good guy now, with
absorbing powers

Echo Echo
Can duplicate into
replicas of himself

Big Chill
This cool guy can
freeze anything

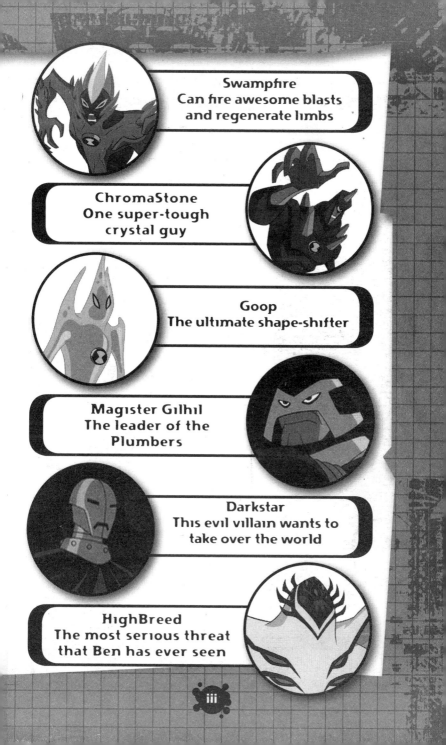

Swampfire
Can fire awesome blasts
and regenerate limbs

ChromaStone
One super-tough
crystal guy

Goop
The ultimate shape-shifter

Magister Gilhil
The leader of the
Plumbers

Darkstar
This evil villain wants to
take over the world

HighBreed
The most serious threat
that Ben has ever seen

EGMONT

We bring stories to life

First published in Great Britain 2010
by Egmont UK Limited
239 Kensington High Street,
London W8 6SA

Adapted by Barry Hutchison

ISBN 978 1 4052 5411 3

1 3 5 7 9 10 8 6 4 2

Printed and bound in Great Britain.

FSC
Mixed Sources
Product group from well-managed
forests and other controlled sources
Cert no. TT-COC-002332
www.fsc.org
© 1996 Forest Stewardship Council

Egmont is passionate about helping to preserve the world's remaining ancient forests.
We only use paper from legal and sustainable forest sources.

This book is made from paper certified by the Forestry Stewardship Council (FSC),
an organisation dedicated to promoting responsible management of forest resources.
For more information on the FSC, please visit www.fsc.org. To learn more about
Egmont's sustainable paper policy, please visit www.egmont.co.uk/ethical

CHAPTER ONE

 UNDER ARREST

A familiar green and black car crept along a city street, its headlights shining brightly in the darkness. Gravel crunched beneath its wheels as the car pulled off the road and rolled to a stop beside an old warehouse.

The engine fell silent and three figures stepped out of the car. They stood close together, looking up at the blacked-out windows of the warehouse.

'Ben, are you sure this is the right place?' asked Kevin, looking around.

Ben nodded. 'That's what the tip said.'

'Yeah, that's what worries me. You don't get tips. I get tips. You've got no connections.'

'C'mon, Kevin,' Ben protested, 'I've got tons of connections.'

'Yeah?' sneered Kevin. 'Like who?'

'Um ...' Ben glanced at his cousin, who was standing just behind Kevin. 'Gwen.'

Gwen nodded, fighting the urge to smile. 'It's true. He does know me.'

'Lot of support there, Gwen,' Ben sighed.

Ignoring her cousin, Gwen began walking towards the warehouse. At the wave of Gwen's hand a series of glowing energy platforms appeared before her, leading up to the roof of the warehouse. She walked up them, with Ben and Kevin following close behind.

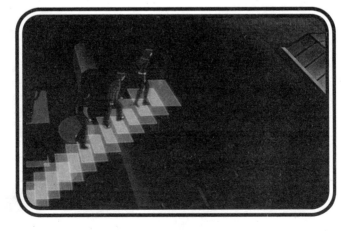

The roof itself was flat, and sturdy enough for them all to walk on. Right in the centre, a raised skylight window allowed them to see what was happening inside. Twenty or more men in silver armour were loading boxes into vans. From where they were standing there was no way of knowing what was in the boxes, but they could guess it was nothing good.

'Forever Knights,' Kevin growled, brushing his hand against the concrete surface of the roof. Almost at once his skin took on the rough grey appearance of the concrete.

'Probably up to no good as usual,' said Gwen, letting sparks of energy crackle across her fingertips.

Beside her, Ben was adjusting the dial on the Omnitrix. He slammed his hand down and an incredible transformation began. Curls of green mist swirled around him as his DNA started to change. His limbs grew longer. His two eyes merged into one. Huge spikes of purple rock grew from his back, until Ben had become the alien known as …

'ChromaStone!'

ChromaStone launched himself up into the air. Tucking his knees up to his chest, he dropped like a stone towards the skylight window.

KA-RAAAASH!

The glass exploded, showering the warehouse with deadly shards. A spider-web pattern of cracks appeared on the concrete floor as ChromaStone's feet slammed hard against it.

A second thud shook the warehouse as Kevin dropped down to join ChromaStone. A second later, Gwen floated down on an energy platform and stood shoulder to shoulder with the rest of the team.

'Nobody move!' bellowed ChromaStone.

Around the heroes, the Forever Knights continued to load up the lorries exactly as they had been doing. None of them even turned to look at the towering alien and his two companions.

'Hey,' said Kevin, 'did you guys hear us?'

Gwen frowned, watching a knight casually wheel a trolley of boxes towards them. 'I don't think so,' she said.

Reaching out a hand, Gwen tried to touch the knight on the arm. Instead, her fingers passed straight through him, as if he wasn't there. They all turned and watched as the knight continued on his way.

'Holograms,' gasped ChromaStone.

'Good guess,' boomed a voice.

With a faint fizzle sound, the knights, trucks and boxes all disappeared, leaving the warehouse empty.

Or almost empty.

A tall, powerfully built figure in futuristic armour stepped out from behind a pillar. He slipped the hologram projector into his utility belt. Most of his face was covered, but an area around his mouth could be seen. The skin was green and as rough as sandpaper. Whoever the man was, he wasn't human.

'Who are you?' demanded ChromaStone. 'Don't come any closer!'

'I am Magister Gilhil of the Plumbers,' he said, introducing himself. 'I'm the commanding officer of this entire quadrant.'

Gilhil took a step closer to the group and slowly raised his Plumber badge. 'You're all under arrest,' he told them, 'for impersonating officers of the law.'

In the blink of an eye ChromaStone transformed back into human form. 'Under arrest for *what?*' Ben demanded.

'Impersonating a Plumber,' Gilhil replied. He was almost double Ben's height and loomed over the boy like a giant. 'We're the only law enforcement organisation recognised by all signatories of the Milky Way treaty. That makes what you've done an interstellar-class felony.'

'Sounds bad,' sneered Kevin, who had barely understood a word the Plumber had said.

Gilhil's mouth pulled into a big scowl. 'Hey, if I were you, kid, I'd keep my mouth in check,' he warned.

Kevin's eyes narrowed. 'If I were you, I wouldn't threaten a guy who could kick your can halfway up the street and back.'

'You feeling froggy, son?' growled Gilhil, clenching his powerful fists. 'Then jump.'

Kevin tensed, but Gwen caught him by the shoulder and held him back. 'If you're feeling smart,' she whispered, 'don't.'

For a moment Kevin hesitated. But only for a moment. Throwing himself at the alien he swung with his solid stone fist. He was going to enjoy pounding on this guy. He was going to –

Kevin barely saw Gilhil move, but the big alien easily caught Kevin's fist in the palm of his hand. With a crack he twisted hard, bending Kevin's wrist backwards. By the time Kevin felt the pain he was already tumbling head-first through the air, straight towards the wall.

KRUNCH!

Kevin thudded against the wall, cracking the plaster. He groaned as he landed heavily on the warehouse floor, but in less than a second he was struggling back to his feet.

Gilhil towered above him. 'Stay down, son,' ordered the alien, but following orders had never been Kevin's style.

Touching the heavy warehouse door, Kevin absorbed its strength. The dull grey of his concrete skin became the shiny silver of metal. If the alien wanted a fight, then Kevin was going to give him one!

Lunging, Kevin swung with his left fist, then his right. Both blows crunched into Gilhil's jaw, stunning him and sending him stumbling backwards. Kevin felt a flash of triumph and prepared to attack again.

'Much as I'd enjoy going a few more rounds with you, I don't have the time,' said Gilhil, pulling a gun from inside his armour.

Before Kevin could react, the alien pulled the trigger. An energy rope launched from the end of the weapon and wrapped itself around Kevin's body, pinning his legs together and binding his hands to his sides. The world seemed to lurch suddenly, as Kevin found himself flipped upside down by the rope and lifted into the air.

Gilhil spun on the spot, pointing his gun at Ben, who was about to activate the Omnitrix. 'Don't,' he warned.

'Do!' cried Gwen, throwing up her hands.

Ben slammed down the Omnitrix's control dial and a cloud of green circled around him. Gilhil's finger twitched on the trigger of his gun, and another energy rope flew at Ben. A crackle of pink energy exploded from Gwen's fingers, blasting the rope to pieces.

Gwen bought her cousin the time he needed. With a gloopy shlopp he transformed into the slimy green alien he called Goop.

Moving like a living puddle, he oozed across the floor and wrapped himself around Gilhil's body, just as the Plumber's rope had done to Kevin.

Gilhil struggled with all his strength, but no matter how hard he wrestled, Goop's grip grew tighter and tighter. With a groan of pain, the Plumber staggered sideways and crashed down onto the floor.

'So you want to talk?' snarled Goop. 'Let's talk!'

CHAPTER TWO

A WARNING

Just a few minutes later, Ben, Gwen and Kevin were standing on the roof. Between them stood Magister Gilhil. He looked angry, but not quite as angry as Kevin.

'I don't see why we gotta talk to him,' Kevin snarled.

'Because I'm the Plumber officer in charge of this whole section of space.'

'Then you know we're the good guys,' said Ben.

Gilhil glared at him. 'What I know is that over the last couple of months, I've gotten several reports of you kids passing yourself off as Plumbers.'

'Our grandfather was a Plumber,' explained Gwen.

'Max Tennyson. He was a good man,'

said Gilhil, fondly. His face hardened again. 'But that doesn't make you Plumbers.' He turned to look at Kevin. 'And you don't even have a claim by blood.'

'Yes I do,' snapped Kevin. 'My father, my real father, was ...' He stopped himself before he could finish the sentence.

Gwen frowned. She'd never heard Kevin talk about his father before. 'Kevin ...?' she asked, gently.

'Nothing,' muttered Kevin, hanging his head. 'Never mind.'

'The point is, there's a reason we shut down Plumber operations on Earth five years ago,' said Gilhil. 'After Vilgax was destroyed –

'Surely you mean after I destroyed him,' smiled Ben.

Gilhil nodded. 'Credit due. But Earth is a backwater Level Two planet. Without an imminent threat, I can't allow Plumber resources to be wasted here. I've got over three hundred inhabited planets under my watch.'

'Look, Magister,' began Ben, stepping forward. 'Can I call you Magister?'

'We met another Plumber called Magister once,' said Gwen. 'Magister Labrid.'

Gilhil snorted with laughter. 'Magister is a rank, not a name. You pretend to be Plumbers but you know nothing about the job.'

'I've never pretended to be anything,' replied Gwen, her voice rising.

'Aliens are attacking our planet. We're just fighting to keep it safe,' said Ben.

The Plumber shook his head. 'I've read a number of reports on your activities. There is no evidence of significant alien activity here.'

'We've seen them!' cried Ben.

Gilhil continued, ignoring Ben's protests. 'I've assigned a new Magister to this region. He'll check in on Earth some time in the next few months. If you have proof, present it to him, and let him take care of Plumber business.'

Ben gasped. 'A few months?'

The huge alien looked around the group, deciding what to do next. 'I'm inclined to give you kids a break,' he said at last. 'Ben, you wear the Omnitrix so you already have special dispensation. The Galvin have requested that you are not interfered with in minor matters.'

Ben was surprised by this. The Galvin were a race of small, super-intelligent aliens. One of them – a scientist named Azmuth – had created the Omnitrix, but Ben always got the feeling that Azmuth didn't like him very much. He was the last person Ben expected to be looking out for him.

Even as Ben thought about this, Gilhil had turned to face Gwen. 'The reports I've read indicate that, as you say, you've never impersonated a Plumber,' he told her. 'But you ...' he began, rounding on Kevin.

'Yeah, what?'

'You've got a record. You've done time in

the Null Void for a variety of crimes.'

'He's changed,' insisted Gwen.

'He's been helping us,' agreed Ben.

'He's been impersonating a Plumber,' Gilhil snapped. He held out a hand that looked strong enough to crush solid rock. 'Give me the badge you stole.'

Kevin's eyes went wide. 'No way. Come on, don't take my badge, man,' he begged, looking to Ben and Gwen for support. 'Please.'

'Now!' demanded Gilhil, 'or you're going back to the Null Void.'

For a moment Kevin hesitated, considering his options. Then, slowly, he reached into his pocket, took out his Plumber badge, and passed it to Gilhil.

'Thank you. You're free to go,' Gilhil announced. 'But if you ever get involved in Plumber business again, you're all going to the Null Void. Even you, Ben.'

The Plumber flicked a switch on his armour and was suddenly surrounded by hundreds of twinkling lights. The lights grew brighter and brighter until, in a sudden flash, Gilhil teleported away.

For several long moments Ben, Gwen and Kevin stood in silence. The only sound was the soft whistling of the breeze and the faint rumbling of distant traffic.

It was Ben who finally said what they were all thinking. 'Is that it?' he asked. 'Is this the end?'

Ben pushed open the door and stepped out of the Mr Smoothy store, sipping from a huge paper cup. Two other cups were balanced on a cardboard tray. Ben slurped down his drink as he strolled across the car park. Eventually he reached Kevin's car. Kevin and Gwen were sat on the bonnet, looking miserable.

'Cheer up,' smiled Ben, before letting out an enormous burp. 'Mr Smoothy makes everything better.'

He handed a cup to Kevin, and one to Gwen. Kevin took a sip, then pulled a disgusted face. 'How does turnip and wheatgrass sludge make anything better?'

SCHLUUURP!

Ben drained the rest of his cup in one go. 'Well, I like it,' he said. 'Besides, it's also got ginger in it.'

Gwen stopped with the straw half-way to her lips. She thought about the ingredients, imagined how they would taste, and then quietly sat her cup down on the ground.

'Oh, ginger,' scowled Kevin. 'Now that solves all our problems.'

'Seriously, Ben,' added Gwen. 'Magister Gilhil pretty much just put us out of business. What are we gonna do?'

Ben hopped up so he was sitting beside his cousin. 'We're gonna keep doing what we've been doing. Find the aliens, fight the bad guys.'

'He said he'd put us in the Null Void,' Gwen reminded him.

'Yeah, but he also said that Plumbers never come around here any more. So we'll worry about it when, or should I say if, he ever shows up again.'

Kevin gave a sigh. 'He took my badge.'

'Badges?' laughed Ben. 'We don't need no stinkin' badges!'

Springing to his feet, Kevin slammed his hand against Ben's chest and caught him by his jacket. 'You think this is a joke?' he growled.

'Kevin, let him go,' cried Gwen.

With a grunt, Kevin released his grip and turned away. 'I wanna be a Plumber, OK?' he mumbled. 'When I was little, my mum would tell me stories about my dad. How he was a Plumber and did all this cool stuff.'

Gwen rested a hand on his shoulder. 'I never met your dad.'

'Me neither,' said Kevin. 'But I still wanna be like him.'

'That's why you know so much about the Plumbers and alien technology and everything,' Gwen realised.

'It's why I agreed to help you guys in the first place.' He turned and looked deep into Gwen's eyes. 'Mostly.'

Gwen opened her mouth to reply, but Kevin had already pulled away. He yanked open the door to his car and climbed inside.

'I've got to get my badge back,' he told them, turning the ignition key and revving the engine. 'It's the only thing that matters.'

Ben barely had time to jump down from the bonnet before Kevin slammed his door shut and hit the accelerator. The car lurched forward and sped off into the distance, leaving Ben and Gwen far behind.

CHAPTER THREE

DARKSTAR ATTACKS

Many miles away from Mr Smoothy, strange alien figures scuttled around a darkened cave, carrying equipment to and from the enormous spaceship that lurked beside them in the dark cavern. They were DNAliens, the servants of the HighBreed.

And they were not alone.

A figure emerged from the shadows, dressed all in black. A metal mask covered his face and head. The mask was blank, aside from two slits for eyes and a larger one for a mouth. As he walked through the cave, a few DNAliens moved to block his path.

The strange figure grabbed the DNAliens and threw them to the ground.

CRASH!

Four of the aliens began to hack and cough. Then, with a horrible retching sound, they spat up football-sized lumps of sticky green goo. The goo-balls shot across the cave, directly towards the masked stranger.

BZZZZZAP!

Powerful blasts of dark energy exploded from the stranger's fingertips. As the blasts hit the goo-balls, they burned up and vanished into dust. The DNAliens began to cough up more gunk, but they were too late. Another blast of dark energy struck the ground by their feet, sending them sprawling backwards onto the cave floor.

Behind his mask, the mysterious stranger smiled. His name was Darkstar, and hurting people was what he did best.

Striding past the unconscious aliens, Darkstar approached the entrance to the spaceship. The thick metal door was closed, but that didn't matter to him. Darkstar had come here for one reason, and nothing was going to get in his way.

Punching his gloved hands against the door frame, Darkstar dug his fingers into the hole his blows created. With a grunt of effort he pulled hard on the door. The metal creaked, then tore free with an ear-splitting crash.

Laser blasts streaked along the spaceship corridor, catching Darkstar by surprise. They hit him in the chest, throwing him backwards and forcing him to throw his hands up in front of his face.

Along the corridor, a squadron of DNAliens advanced, squeezing the triggers of their laser guns, blasting the intruder again and again. They communicated anxiously in their alien language, shouting to make themselves heard above the screaming of their weapons.

Darkstar didn't know what the aliens were saying and he didn't care. They had taken him by surprise, but he had recovered quickly. They were no longer a threat to him. They were simply annoying.

With a flick of his wrist he sent bolts of energy screeching towards the oncoming aliens. The blasts moved too quickly for the DNAliens to dodge them. Several voices cried out in pain. Several guns clattered to the ground. And then there was no sound in the corridor, but the soft thudding of Darkstar's footsteps.

Half-way along the corridor, Darkstar heard another sound. It was soft and faint and coming from directly above him. Reaching up with one hand, he caught the DNAlien who had been preparing to leap down on top of him. Without even slowing down, he slammed the creature head-first against the ground, and turned the corner at the corridor's end.

More DNAliens lay in wait, their weapons raised and ready to fire. Darkstar sighed. This was becoming boring. Very boring. Raising his hands he unleashed a rain of dark energy. In less than a second, not a single alien was left standing.

Stepping over their bodies, Darkstar approached the door they had been guarding. Behind his mask his eyes blazed with excitement. This was it. This was the moment he had been waiting for.

The metal door collapsed with a single shove, and the masked figure stepped through the hole that was left in its place. Across the room a high-backed chair spun around, revealing a HighBreed alien.

'Who are you?' demanded the alien, leaping to his feet. 'And what insignificant alien speck dares to enter the command centre of a HighBreed Lord?'

He was easily twice as tall as Darkstar, and from the way he spoke it was obvious that he was very angry.

Darkstar didn't reply. Instead he kept walking, each step bringing him closer and closer to the hulking alien.

'It doesn't matter,' snorted the HighBreed. 'Dead men don't need names.'

THWACK!

A crunching back-hand caught Darkstar on the side of the head and sent him crashing into a bank of computer monitors. The equipment exploded beneath him, bringing a mound of rock and broken metal down on top of his head.

Darkstar got to his feet, brushing the heavy equipment away as if it were made of cardboard. 'Nice shot,' he said, picking up a heavy boulder and raising it above his head. 'You're just as strong as I'd heard.'

The HighBreed braced himself for battle, but his opponent was already on the attack. Darkstar hurled the boulder with all his strength. It flipped twice in the air, then found its target. The HighBreed roared in pain and rage as he was knocked to the ground.

But the alien wasn't beaten yet. Pushing

the rock aside he began to climb to his feet, his diamond-shaped eyes fixed on his enemy. The HighBreed tensed his huge muscles, preparing to fight.

Beneath his mask, Darkstar licked his lips. 'That's it,' he hissed, raising his hand. 'Show me all of your power!'

A band of black energy snaked from Darkstar's fingertips. It wrapped around the HighBreed and seemed to burrow through the alien's skin.

'Give me your strength.'

The HighBreed howled and thrashed around as Darkstar drained the power from his body. He tried to fight, but he was weakening too quickly. With a final cry of pain, the huge alien collapsed, face first, to the ground.

After taking a moment to enjoy the taste of the HighBreed's powerful energy, Darkstar crossed to the fallen alien and poked him with the toe of his boot. The HighBreed rolled over onto his back and groaned.

'What do you want from me?'

Darkstar crouched down so his mask was just a few centimetres away from the alien's face. 'I want,' he said, 'to make a deal.'

Kevin twisted the spanner, tightening a part of his car's engine that had been tight enough to begin with. There was nothing wrong with the car, but he liked tinkering with it. It helped him to think.

He was so busy thinking he almost didn't hear the footsteps approaching his garage until it was too late.

'Who's out there?' he growled, peering out into the darkness beyond the garage door.

For a moment nothing happened, and then Gwen appeared, a plastic cup in each hand. 'Me,' she said with a smile. 'I brought you something to drink.'

Kevin shuddered. 'Yeah, but no thanks. I'm fine.'

'It's not a smoothie,' Gwen said, taking a sip from one of the cups. 'See? Regular soda.'

She held the cup out to Kevin. He hesitated for a moment, before taking it from her. 'OK,' he said, before taking a long drink.

'I just wanted to see how you were doing,' said Gwen.

'Fine,' Kevin took a deep breath. 'Listen, I don't want to talk about my dad.'

'Never crossed my mind,' Gwen replied. 'I brought you a present.' She pulled a small bag from her pocket. Reaching inside she pulled out a small ball and tossed it to Kevin.

'What's this?' he asked, catching the ball and studying it.

'A wooden ball. Absorb it.'

Kevin shrugged and absorbed the

properties of the ball. At once his hand became a dark shade of brown.

'How about this one?' asked Gwen, throwing him another. 'It's a ball bearing. Made out of, I dunno, ball bearing stuff.'

'Stainless steel.'

'I brought you a whole bag of them, all made of different materials,' Gwen told him. 'That way, when we're in a fight, you can change to whatever you want.'

'Thanks, but it doesn't really work that way,' replied Kevin, taking the bag. 'I need a lot of whatever I'm copying.'

Gwen looked disappointed. 'Oh.'

'And what makes you think I'm still helping you guys, anyway?'

Taking Kevin's hand, Gwen said, 'Because you've changed.'

'Maybe, but I'm still on parole. That Magister can put me back in the Null Void any time he wants.'

Gwen held Kevin's hand tighter. There was so much she wanted to say to him. If only she could show him how important he was to the team – and to her.

KARAAASH!

A sudden shattering of stone derailed Gwen's train of thought. She and Kevin spun around to face the wall. A large area of brickwork had been torn away. In its place stood the hulking frame of the HighBreed Lord.

'Human scum,' the alien squealed, 'I will cleanse the world of your filth!'

Placing his hands against the floor, Kevin quickly absorbed the properties of the concrete. As his body became as hard as stone, he turned to Gwen. 'Looks like I picked the wrong day to give up fighting monsters.'

CHAPTER FOUR

FRAMED

I t's a HighBreed!' cried Gwen. 'Ben says
they're too strong for us to fight.'

'Well, Ben ain't here!'

Kevin darted forwards, his fists clenched.
The alien was much taller than he was, and he
had to leap upwards to drive two solid punches
against the HighBreed's jaw. But the alien
barely seemed to notice them.

THWACK!

Lashing out, the HighBreed hit Kevin with a powerful uppercut, sending him backflipping across the garage. With a crash of metal, Kevin smashed into the bonnet of his car, crumpling it. Groaning, Kevin tried to get up, but his arms shook, then folded beneath him.

Stepping in front of her fallen friend, Gwen hit the HighBreed with an energy beam. The pink light wrapped itself around the alien, tightening like a rope around its body.

With a shrug of powerful shoulders, the HighBreed shook off the energy beam, sending it rocketing back towards Gwen. Ducking too late, Gwen caught the blast on the side of her head. The world seemed to spin for a moment, before Gwen sunk to the floor, her eyes closed.

Fighting to stay awake, Gwen forced her eyes open again, just in time to see the HighBreed slamming his fists down towards her. Gasping, she threw up an energy shield, just in time to stop the alien crushing her.

'That won't save you, human!' roared the HighBreed, raining blow after deadly blow down on the shield.

Gwen's eyes went wide with horror as the shield began to crack beneath the strain. Finally, with one last punch, the shield flickered and disappeared. The HighBreed cackled loudly as he brought his huge fist down one last time. Gwen screwed her eyes tight shut, bracing herself for the end.

KRUUUNCH!

Gwen opened her eyes again and found herself looking into Kevin's. He kneeled over her, shielding her from the HighBreed's punch. For a moment he tried to smile, and then his eyes rolled back in his head and his rock covering began to crack and crumble.

With a final whimper of pain, Kevin rolled sideways and lay still on the garage floor. Gwen looked up, defenceless now as the HighBreed raised his fists to deliver the final killer blow.

And then, without warning, a hand – even bigger than the alien's – caught the HighBreed by the wrist.

'Hey, ugly,' growled Humungousaur. 'Why don't you pick on somebody your own size?'

Humungousaur spun quickly on the spot, keeping a tight grip on the HighBreed's wrist. Faster and faster the alien hero turned, until he was spinning at just the perfect speed.

With a grunt, Humungousaur launched

the HighBreed up towards the garage ceiling. The roof exploded, showering glass, stone and dust up into the night sky.

Screaming, the HighBreed tumbled through the air, before finally crashing back down to earth with the force of a small meteorite, creating a deep crater in the ground.

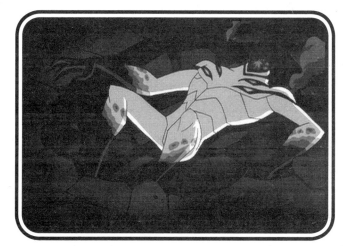

At the bottom of the crater, the HighBreed wiped dust from his eyes. His whole body hurt, but that would not stop him. He began to get to his feet. Nothing would stop him. Nothing!

An angry, dinosaur-like face glared down at him from the top of the pit. 'I wouldn't, if I were you,' growled Humungousaur.

The HighBreed swallowed hard. OK, so maybe that would stop him.

Gwen and Kevin – who were both now back on their feet – rushed over to join Humungousaur at the edge of the crater. If the HighBreed decided to keep fighting, then they wanted a piece of the action too.

A voice from nearby took them by surprise. 'Didn't take you kids long to get yourselves into trouble again, did it?'

Humungousaur and the others turned to find Magister Gilhil watching them.

'We were just – ' Humungousaur began.

'Attacking me for no reason,' finished the HighBreed, clambering free of the crater.

'He's one of the aliens we told you about,' argued Kevin. 'He's attacking Earth.'

'How about some proof?' sighed Gilhil.

'They attacked me for no reason,' insisted the HighBreed. 'They said they were Plumbers.'

Gilhil's eyes darkened. 'I've heard enough. You three are under arrest. And you,' he said, turning to the HighBreed, 'I don't know what's going on here, but I'm gonna find out. You're coming with me for questioning.'

'I beg to differ,' boomed another voice. This time it was Darkstar's turn to make a surprise appearance. 'Nobody's going anywhere,' he told them. 'Not until I make your powers my own!'

The night air seemed to sizzle as the dark energy snaked from Darkstar's fingertips. Five bolts shot out, four of them hitting their targets. Only Gwen was fast enough to surround herself with an energy bubble. All around her, the others fell to the ground, writhing in pain as Darkstar drained them of their strength.

'Why me?' cried the HighBreed. 'You promised that if I helped you ...'

Behind his mask, Darkstar's mouth pulled into a sneer. 'I can't be trusted,' he laughed.

Humungousaur gritted his teeth. He'd never felt such pain before. On his left, Kevin was already knocked out. On his right, Gilhil was also falling unconscious. Gwen was pinned inside her energy bubble. That left only him.

Summoning all his strength, the huge dino-alien took a step towards Darkstar. The pain became worse, but he couldn't give up. He wouldn't. Another step brought him closer to the masked figure. Then another, and another.

'I'd almost forgotten how strong you are,' said Darkstar, shouting to make himself heard over the buzzing of his energy beams. 'Ben.'

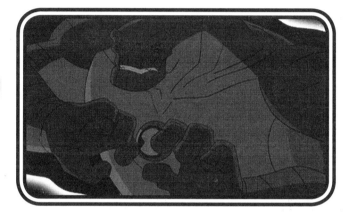

Spreading his fingers wider, he increased the power of his beams. Humungousaur roared in pain. Then in a blur of green, the alien transformed back into Ben.

'Who are you?' Ben gasped, his power still being sapped by Darkstar. 'How did you – ?'

And then, in a blinding flash, the truth hit him. Ben knew now who he was dealing with, and it made his blood run cold.

'Gwen, run!' he cried.

'What?'

'You've got to get away, you're our only hope. Run!'

Gwen hesitated. She didn't like the idea of running out on the others, but there was no way she could stop Darkstar on her own.

With a final glance down at Kevin, Gwen bunched her energy shield up into a ball and sent it rocketing towards Darkstar. It exploded in a blinding light around him.

By the time Darkstar's vision had cleared, Gwen was nowhere to be seen.

'You can't run forever, lovely Gwen,' he shouted. 'I'll have my revenge on you, too!'

Darkstar turned and looked down at the four other figures, who were all lying on the ground. A glint lit up his eyes as his gaze fell on Ben and Kevin. 'But first things first ...'

CHAPTER FIVE

UNEXPECTED ALLIES

Ben forced open his eyes and immediately wished that he hadn't. He was tied with heavy chains and pinned inside a glowing blue energy prison, unable to move. Judging by the equipment around the room, the prison seemed to be inside a power plant, but he couldn't say for sure. Beside him, Kevin, Gilhil and the HighBreed were trapped in the same way.

'I don't understand what's going on,' groaned Gilhil. 'That's the guy who tipped me off that you were impersonating Plumbers.'

Kevin grunted. 'And he scammed big ugly, too.'

The HighBreed growled at him.

'I know who he is,' Ben announced.

'Do you really?' boomed Darkstar, who had been standing nearby, watching on.

'You have to be somebody who knows all about the Plumbers and the HighBreed,' Ben replied. 'But most importantly, you have to be someone with a grudge against us. Why don't you take off the dopey mask, Mike?'

'That's Mike Morningstar?' splutted Kevin. 'The creep who tried to steal Gwen from ...' He stopped just in time to avoid saying anything embarrassing. 'Who stole his powers from all those girls at his school?'

'When you ruined my plan, you nearly destroyed me,' Darkstar said. 'But my powers returned, stronger than ever. As did my hunger. My old method of feeding is not enough.'

'High school girls too tough for you, huh?' snorted Ben.

'To the contrary, my friends. I need more power than they can supply. Mike Morningstar no longer exists.'

With a clatter his metal mask fell to the floor. Ben and Kevin stared in disbelief at the horror standing before them. Mike's once handsome features were now shrivelled and decayed, his skin wrinkled and grey.

'Now I am Darkstar!' he said, enjoying his enemies' horrified reaction. 'You did this to me. And you will feed my hunger.'

More of Darkstar's energy beams shot from his hands. They passed easily through the force field and wrapped around the four prisoners. The captives cried out in pain.

'I will take your strength and make it my own, until you have no more to give.'

Kevin fought against the pain. 'Ben, if you can reach your Omnitrix,' he mumbled, 'maybe Alien X – '

Ben shook his head. 'No. If he absorbed all that power, nothing could stop him.'

'Eventually, I'll have it all anyway,' said Darkstar, grinning.

From close behind him, Darkstar heard a faint cough. He turned around, only to find Gwen standing inside the doorway. She was leaning against the wall, her arms folded.

'Ew,' winced Gwen, when she saw Darkstar's face. 'I swear you were better looking when we used to go out.'

'Laugh while you can,' Darkstar hissed. 'I've got all the power of your teammates, plus the HighBreed and the Plumber. How can you possibly hope to defeat me alone?'

Gwen raised an eyebrow. 'Who said anything about "alone"?'

As if on cue, the windows of the room exploded inwards, as dozens of DNAliens came crashing through. Yet more of them swarmed in through the door behind Gwen.

'They're pretty mad at you for kidnapping their boss,' said Gwen, just as the first wave of DNAliens launched an attack on Darkstar. Darkstar reacted quickly, knocking them back with an energy blast. But another group were already launching a second assault, forcing Darkstar to fire wildly as he struggled to keep them all back.

From across the room Gwen fired an energy beam of her own. It hit the force field projector, frying the electrics inside. The prison walls flickered for a moment, then disappeared.

Absorbing the metal of the chains around him, Kevin turned his body into living iron. Flexing his metallic muscles he snapped the chain, and set about freeing Ben and Gilhil.

'Thanks, kid,' said the Plumber as his chains were torn away.

'What about me?' said the HighBreed.

'Hang in there,' said Ben with a smirk.

Just a few metres away, Darkstar was grappling with a DNAlien. Placing his hand against its head he drained its energy away. The power tasted good, but the aliens had surrounded him and were moving in to attack.

'Too many to absorb,' he muttered.

'And the bad news keeps on coming,' said Gwen, raising her hands.

A circle of pink energy thundered into Darkstar, sending him tumbling into the wall. He was spinning too fast to notice the flash of green energy as Ben transformed into the alien known as Echo Echo.

Opening his mouth wide, Echo Echo hit Darkstar with a sonic blast, catapulting him high up into the air. Gilhil drew his weapon and took aim. With a squeeze of the trigger he blasted Darkstar with a laser bolt, taking some of the fight out of him.

But Darkstar wasn't done yet. He raised his arms, preparing to unleash his dark energy. From the corner of his eye he spotted a burst of green light, and turned just in time to see Spidermonkey swinging towards him.

Spidermonkey's feet slammed hard against Darkstar's jaw, sending him plummeting towards the ground. Even as Spidermonkey fell after him, the Omnitrix energy swirled around, changing him into yet another alien form.

Jet Ray raised his tail and fired a stream of green energy at Darkstar, blasting him just as he crunched against the concrete floor.

Weakened, but determined to win the fight, Darkstar tried to get to his feet. Before he could get very far, an enormous shadow loomed over him. Collapsing onto his back, he looked up at the snarling face of Humungousaur.

'Nighty-night,' growled the dino-alien, raising a massive foot.

BADOOOM!

Humungousaur brought his foot down on the fallen figure of Darkstar – not hard enough to kill him, but hard enough to make sure he wouldn't be getting back up any time soon.

With Darkstar finally defeated, Gwen

glanced over to where they had left the HighBreed Lord. Only his chains remained.

'The HighBreed is gone,' she sighed.

'The DNAliens must have sprung him while we were fighting,' said Kevin, turning back into his human form. He looked across to Humungousaur, just in time to see him transform back to Ben. 'You OK, man?'

Ben shook his head. 'Tired,' he gasped, before falling to his knees. Gwen caught him.

'Sit down and catch your breath,' she said, guiding him gently to the ground.

Gilhil leaned closer. 'Is he OK?'

'Everything ... spinning. Double vision. Going dim,' Ben groaned. 'Need ... smoothie.'

Gwen smiled, relieved. 'He's fine.'

Less than an hour later, all four of the heroes stood outside the power station. Darkstar stood between them, trapped inside an energy prison, his hands bound by laser cuffs.

'Will that rig hold him?' asked Kevin.

'It's Level Six technology,' Gilhil replied. 'He isn't going anywhere but the Null Void.'

'What about us?' asked Ben.

'I've been giving that some thought. You guys made a difference today. Maybe I don't need to reassign good men to this quadrant,' said Gilhil. 'Maybe they're already here.'

Kevin frowned. 'What's that mean?'

'You've been drafted. Here's your badge back.' Gilhil held out a Plumber badge. Kevin took it eagerly. 'And here's one for you,' said Gilhil, passing a badge to Gwen. Ben held out his hand. 'Don't push it, kid. You've already got the Omnitrix.'

Ben couldn't argue with that.

'As of now you're the only law in the quadrant,' Gilhil told them. Lights twinkled around him and Darkstar as they began to teleport away. 'Do a good job.'

And with that, the Plumber vanished. Ben turned to look at his friends, but Kevin was already walking away.

'Hey, where are you going?'

Kevin glanced back at the others, then looked down at the badge. His badge. He smiled. 'I gotta tell my mum.'

Goop gets Magister Gilhil in
one gooey trap

Gwen and Kevin prepare to battle

The evil Darkstar is on a
mission for power

But the DNAliens put up a fight

Gwen uses her awesome force field

Ben slams down his Omnitrix

Darkstar zaps some
beams at his prisoners

But Jet Ray sends some red-hot
lasers his way!

Ben transforms into Echo Echo

Echo Echo gets sucked into
the teleporter with a HighBreed

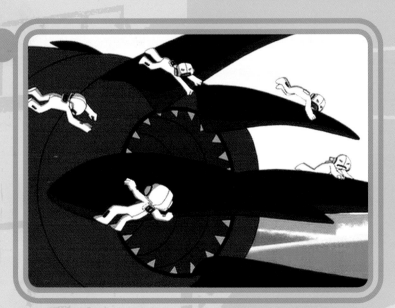

An evil Dravek means trouble

Swampfire and the HighBreed
work together

The desolate planet is burning hot

Big Chill turns the
temperature right down

A swarm of Dasypodidae start an attack

But Swampfire scorches them with flamebolts!

CHAPTER ONE

GONE

Laser blasts erupted around Ben's head, blasting holes in the wall behind him. Ducking behind a stack of boxes, he spun the dial on the Omnitrix, keeping one eye on the HighBreed who had been shooting at him.

The towering alien turned and launched a bundle of deadly spikes towards Gwen, who was taking cover behind a pillar. She waited for them to clatter to the floor before risking a glance at the HighBreed.

'It's trying to run,' she yelled. 'Cut it off!'

Kevin launched himself from one of the warehouse's many shadows, landing heavily on the HighBreed's back. He fired a punch against the side of its head, but if the alien felt it he didn't show it. With a twitch of his shoulders he threw Kevin into a stack of wooden boxes.

'I've got it covered,' Ben cried, making straight for the HighBreed and slapping a hand down hard against the face of the Omnitrix. The Omnitrix projected a bright green light across the warehouse. In a flash Ben transformed into the alien form known as Echo Echo.

Still running, Echo Echo split into six identical clones of himself. Together they surrounded the HighBreed, cutting off his escape. 'Going somewhere? I don't think so!' they all said at once.

The HighBreed raised both fists above his head and then slammed them down against the stone floor. As the ground shook, the six Echo Echoes were thrown backwards, off balance.

Shrieking, Gwen hurled five energy balls at the HighBreed, one after another. They hit him hard, staggering him enough for Kevin to rush in and land a punch. In his stone form, Kevin was strong – really strong. The force of the punch lifted the HighBreed off his feet. The ground shook again as he landed on his back with a thump.

Kevin picked up one of the Echo Echoes and scowled at him. 'Nice going Mr "I've got it covered". Not much help there.'

'Hey, I'm all over it!' chimed the clones, sprinting past Kevin to where the HighBreed was getting to his feet. The clones swarmed all over the enormous alien, holding onto his arms and legs and wrapping their stubby arms tightly around his head.

'Don't touch me, creature,' spat the HighBreed, squirming as he tried to shake the little aliens off. As he struggled, his eyes fell on a large piece of machinery that was half-hidden in the corner of the warehouse. Slowly, he dragged himself towards it.

'Don't let him get in that thing,' barked Kevin. 'It's a teleporter pod.'

Bending, Kevin tore a chunk of concrete from the floor and hurled it towards the teleporter. It struck the side of the machine and an explosion of blue sparks fizzed from inside the control panel.

'You've damaged the transmission field, you stupid human!' roared the HighBreed. Still wrestling with the six Echo Echo clones, he tried to turn. A big flash of blue energy hit him like a lightning bolt. He felt his feet slip from under him.

The HighBreed's scream echoed around

the warehouse as the blue light became blindingly bright. Gwen and Kevin shielded their eyes unable to look at the glow.

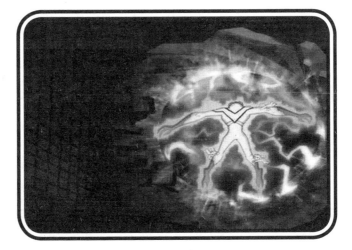

They opened their eyes just in time to see the HighBreed – with the Echo Echoes still holding onto him – being sucked into the teleporter. The machine shook violently for a moment, before becoming still. The blue glow faded to darkness.

'Ben!' cried Kevin.

But Ben was gone.

One by one the Echo Echo clones landed heavily on the sandy ground of a barren desert. The HighBreed alien loomed above them, his fists clenched.

'Microcephalic, vermin-ridden carcass,' he bellowed.

The Echo Echoes leapt to their feet. 'That's an insult, right?' they asked.

'Your friend interfered with the teleporter settings. He is a fool.'

'Well, to be fair, we were more than a little distracted,' replied Echo Echo. 'What with you trying to kill us and all.'

'That's right, I was,' nodded the HighBreed. 'In fact, I still am.'

He swung down at the closest clone with

a punch that would surely have knocked its head clean off. But Echo Echo was fast.

He dodged left, out of harm's way, then opened his mouth and hit the HighBreed with a sonic scream.

The HighBreed skidded backwards across the sand, stunned but not hurt. He was about to attack again when he felt a tremor underneath him. Then the entire desert started to rumble.

Echo Echo frowned. 'Whoa. Um … was that an earthquake?'

The HighBreed was about to answer when he felt the ground move beneath his feet. He threw himself out of the way just as a giant, worm-like head erupted from the sand.

'This isn't good,' Echo Echo muttered.

The worm-creature pushed up and up, stretching from the ground until it stood as tall as a skyscraper. Echo Echo peered up at him.

'Whoa,' he cried, 'think I'm gonna need some back-up here!'

In a blur of green, Echo Echo split into a dozen more copies of himself. They all looked up in time to see the worm creature diving towards them, its gaping mouth wide open.

'Now let's try this again!' they yelled, opening their own mouths almost as wide as the monster's. Working as one they blasted the worm with their sonic screams. The creature thrashed around for a few moments, then slammed its head against the sand and burrowed back below ground.

The desert fell deadly silent, but not for long. A few seconds later, the ground beneath

Echo Echo's feet began to tremble.

'Not good, not good!' the clones chimed.

KRRRRAAAAWK!

The worm-creature's head burst through the ground directly below one of the clones. It flashed its pointed teeth, then swallowed the Echo Echo whole!

The other clones watched on, horrified, unsure of what to do next. Suddenly, the worm-creature began to gag and choke. With a final splutter he coughed up the Echo Echo clone, sending him rocketing towards the others. The little alien collided with his fellow clones, knocking them down like skittles.

The worm-creature then turned and fixed his gaze on the HighBreed. The little creature had not tasted good. Perhaps the larger one would taste better!

'HighBreed, look out! Run!' cried Echo Echo, as the giant worm began to race after the fleeing HighBreed.

As he darted across the desert, the HighBreed turned and fired energy bolts up at his pursuer. The worm-creature didn't even slow down.

Merging back into a single being, Echo Echo hopped up onto the worm's tail and raced along its slimy back. When he was somewhere near the head, he took a deep breath and unleashed a sonic scream. This time he focused the full strength of the blast at where he guessed the monster's brain would be.

The worm shrieked loudly and began to thrash around in pain on the sand. Seizing his chance, the HighBreed fired one energy bolt after another, concentrating on the spot Echo Echo was attacking.

As the blasts struck the worm, it decided enough was enough. Echo Echo only just managed to leap from the monster's back, before it buried itself deep back into the sandy desert floor.

'What was that thing?' asked Echo Echo, when he was sure the creature had gone.

'A Dravek. Its kind is numerous on this deadly planet.'

Echo Echo nodded. 'Then we'd better get off this planet before any more of them show up. We don't want to bump into one of those in the night!'

The HighBreed scowled. 'We? What exactly do you mean by "we", filthy human?'

'Yes, dear HighBreed – "we",' replied Echo Echo. 'You couldn't defeat it alone, and I couldn't defeat it alone. If more of them come our only hope of survival is if we fight together!'

CHAPTER TWO

AN UNEASY ALLIANCE

From the HighBreed's body language Echo Echo could tell he was disgusted at the very idea of them working together.

'You know I'm right,' the little alien said.

'I know no such thing,' the HighBreed repiled.

Echo Echo shrugged. He didn't enjoy the idea of working with the HighBreed, but he'd enjoy being eaten by a Dravek even less. 'I don't like this any better than you do,' he said.

Looking past the HighBreed he spotted for the first time that there were two suns in the sky. No wonder the place was so hot.

'Um, how do we get off this, um, planet-whatever-it's-called?'

'We are on Turrawuste, a desert world,

useful only as a teleporter relay station,' the HighBreed told him.

'So how come we didn't beam in near the teleporter machine?'

'The damage to the pod must have temporarily shifted the focusing axis.'

'Can you fix it?'

The HighBreed growled. 'If we find the teleporter pod on this planet, we won't need to fix it,' he said. 'Simply avoid hitting it with a rock while it is activated.'

'OK, smart guy,' replied Echo Echo. 'Where is it?'

'Impossible to tell.'

'Impossible for you, maybe.' Echo Echo opened his mouth wider than ever before and let out a deafening sonic shriek. He listened to it roll off into the distance. Then, very faintly, he heard a soft ping as the sonar detected something metal.

'That way,' Echo Echo said, pointing in

the direction of the sound. 'It'll take a day or more to reach it on foot. Let's go.'

He began to walk, but quickly realised the HighBreed wasn't following.

'C'mon, alien dude, the sooner we get moving, the sooner we get home,' said Ben. 'Then we'll both be happy.'

'Your kind disgusts me,' seethed the HighBreed.

'Huh? What did you say?'

'I will not allow such a filthy creature to spend a single moment longer in my presence.'

'Creeps you out? Hey, I can take care of that. Watch this.'

With a flash, Echo Echo transformed back into Ben. 'See? I'm really just a plain ol' human.'

'That is even worse!' bellowed the HighBreed. 'Be gone, foul thing. I shall traverse to the teleporter alone.'

Suddenly, the roar of a Dravek boomed across the sand. It sounded far away, but close enough to be worrying.

'We have to watch each other's backs,' said Ben. 'We don't want any more Draveks to drop in on us. Or under us. If you know what I mean ...'

Yet again, the HighBreed made no sign of moving. He turned his head sharply.

'Now what?' Ben sighed.

'If I am forced to travel with you, then you must keep ten paces behind me at all times.'

'But I'm the one who knows the way,' Ben reminded him.

'Ten paces!'

Ben shook his head and sighed. 'Fine. Whatever. Just get moving.'

Satisfied, the HighBreed started walking. Ben counted ten paces, shook his head again, then set off across the desert.

The planet's twin suns blazed down on them and scorched the sand beneath their feet as they slowly made their way towards the distant teleporter.

Wiping the sweat from his forehead, Ben joked, 'Phew! Hot enough for you?'

'Yes.'

'No, see, I wasn't really asking,' said Ben. 'It's just an expression. It means it's hot out.'

'It is obviously hot,' spat the HighBreed. 'I do not see the point of reiterating what we both already know.'

'Sheesh,' said Ben. 'Makes me glad I didn't say "it's not the heat, it's the humidity".'

'There is no humidity,' the big alien snapped. 'It is, in fact, the heat.'

'I know,' Ben mumbled. 'Just trying to make conversation.'

Then without warning, the HighBreed stumbled and fell forwards onto the sand. Ben rushed over to see what was wrong.

'Do not lay your hands on me, vile thing,' barked the HighBreed as Ben approached.

Ben hesitated, then quickly removed his jacket and held it out for the alien. 'Here, you can use this to keep the sun off your head. It'll help to protect you.'

The HighBreed knocked the jacket away. 'I do not take charity from vermin. I merely require a moment's rest.'

'Rest won't cut it, I'm afraid. You're dehydrated already.'

'The one true species thrives in a much cooler climate.'

'Humans like it cooler than this, too. But you're actually wasting away here. I've got something that can help us both beat the heat. Hang on.'

SLAM!

Ben smacked his hand against the face of the Omnitrix. A familiar green glow wrapped itself around him, changing him into another of his alien forms.

'Big Chill!' he cried, unfurling his wide, moth-like wings and springing up into the air.

'What are you doing, foul creature?' the HighBreed hissed. 'Stay away from me.'

'Hey, I'm watching your back, dude,' Big Chill replied, hovering over the HighBreed. 'It's time to cool down!'

Taking a deep breath, Big Chill suddenly blasted out a cloud of icy cold air across the HighBreed's back.

'Desist,' said the HighBreed, weakly. 'Stop that this instant.'

Big Chill stopped blowing. 'Why?'

'I did not request your assistance.'

'I know. Chill, dude.' His mouth curved into a wide grin. 'Ha! See what I did there?'

'I do not.'

'I made a little pun,' smiled Big Chill. 'See, I ... hey, what's that?' Big Chill's smile slowly faded as he stared off across the desert, to where a patch of blue liquid was shimmering in the sand. 'Water!'

'Your powers of deduction are truly staggering,' said the HighBreed, sarcastically.

'Uh, whatever. I'm going to get a drink,' announced Big Chill, fluttering off in the direction of the water pool. 'I'll bring some back for you.'

Landing softly beside the oasis, Big Chill reached out a hand. The "water" felt warm and slimy to the touch. He sniffed it, trying to work out what it was. The smell was familiar – he'd smelled it only recently.

Oh no!

Big Chill suddenly remembered where he had smelled this stuff before. Inside the Dravek.

He spun around in time to see the jagged teeth of the worm-creature rise up from beneath the sand all around him. The liquid wasn't water, it was saliva. He'd flown straight into a Dravek's trap!

As the teeth closed in around him, Big Chill launched himself skyward. Using his alien abilities he passed through the teeth as if he were a ghost. He emerged on the other side, leaving a layer of thick ice over the worm-creature's mouth.

While the Dravek shook off the ice, Big Chill flew back to the HighBreed. 'It was a trap,' he told him.

Huge chunks of ice began to fall away from the Dravek's mouth.

'That thing's getting loose,' warned Big Chill. 'Come on – we've got to move.'

'You cannot issue commands to me, mongrel. Lesser beings do my bidding. You will do as I say.' The HighBreed stood up just as the Dravek shook off the last of the ice from its huge mouth. It began to squirm in their direction, showing its razor-sharp teeth. The HighBreed then turned to Big Chill. 'I bid you to fight.'

'Oh, all right then. If you say so!' said Big Chill, wrapping up in an invisible cloak.

Beating his wings, Big Chill raced over to the Dravek and phased through its body. At the alien's touch, a layer of ice began to spread across the worm-creature's skin.

KERAAACK!

Twisting its body, the Dravek shattered the ice into fragments. As the pieces hit the sand they began to melt almost at once. Big Chill launched another attack. This time, he hit the monster right in its eyes, but the Dravek shattered the ice immediately.

'It's not working!' Big Chill cried, as the

Dravek shook off yet another ice blast.

Roaring in triumph, the Dravek pulled itself up to its full height, opened its mouth, and prepared to strike.

CHAPTER THREE

'We can't keep this up much longer,' hissed Big Chill.

'Follow my lead,' barked the HighBreed.

'And do what?'

'Freeze him.'

'Already tried that.'

'From inside,' the HighBreed said. 'Stay inside. Keep him frozen until I say otherwise.'

Big Chill didn't much like the idea of hanging about in the Dravek's insides, but there was no time for argument. Flying upwards he disappeared inside the creature's mouth and raced down its throat.

The HighBreed watched as the worm-creature began to slow. Its red skin went a dark shade of blue, before crystals of white ice began to form on the surface. In just a few moments the entire worm was encased in a shell of thick white frost.

'Now!' the HighBreed bellowed, raising both hands high up into the air. As Big Chill phased, ghost-like, from within the beast, the HighBreed fired twenty or more pointed spikes up into the ice.

The frozen worm started to vibrate. Then it let out an ear-splitting roar. The ice shattered into a thousand little pieces and the Dravek retreated back underground.

The HighBreed sunk back down onto the baking hot desert floor. He was boiling hot. Big Chill knew he had to help the HighBreed cool down. Taking a deep breath, he got ready with another blast of cold air.

'Don't you dare,' the HighBreed seethed. 'Leave me be. Now that the danger has passed, I can locate water myself.'

A flap of skin on the alien's chest pulled back, making way for two long tendrils. The tendrils looked like the roots of a plant, but wriggled like snakes as they burrowed deep down into the sand.

'Ew,' Big Chill muttered. 'Gross.'

'There is water below the sand, if one looks deep enough,' the HighBreed said. Just then, liquid began to bubble up from where his tendrils had entered the ground. 'There.'

'I didn't know you HighBreeds were some kind of plant.'

'We are not "some kind" of anything.

The HighBreed is the only kind.'

And with that, he began to drink.

A few minutes later, Ben was finishing the last of the water. It tasted better than anything he had ever drunk before, and he could already feel some of his strength returning.

The HighBreed, too, looked much stronger. He was up on his feet, resuming the march towards the teleporter. Ben was about to follow when he heard a faint scratching sound.

'Did you hear something?' Ben asked, glancing at the ground around them.

Ten paces in front, the HighBreed didn't bother looking back. 'I heard nothing. Except you, human. Which is the same as nothing.'

'Ha. Ha,' Ben said, not laughing.

'I believe I am beginning to grasp your

concept of "humour".' He was about to continue when the ground beneath him trembled. The HighBreed stopped, his muscles tensed.

'Uh oh. More Draveks underground?' whispered Ben.

The HighBreed shook his head. 'Worse.'

'C'mon,' gulped Ben. 'Worse?'

From behind them the scratching sound came again. Ben whipped around and gasped at what he saw. An area of desert about the size of a football pitch was moving as if it were alive. As Ben and the HighBreed watched, thousands of armoured creepy crawlies scurried from beneath the sand.

'Dasypodidae,' said the HighBreed, recognising the creatures.

'They're little,' smiled Ben. 'How could these guys possibly be worse than Draveks?'

The answer came right away. Dozens of the little bugs clambered up Ben's legs and over his body, almost covering him completely. He thrashed around, trying to shake them away.

'Get them off me!'

The HighBreed was in no position to help. Hundreds of the Dasypodidae were scurrying all over him, dragging him to the ground. He and Ben both fell at the same time, and were quickly covered by a living carpet of the killer insects.

A burst of bright green light briefly illuminated the heaving mass, as Ben transformed into Swampfire.

'This'll only take a second,' he said, hurling huge fireballs down towards the bugs. His eyes flicked up and he realised there were several thousand more rushing in to replace the ones he had burned. 'Did I say a second? I'm now thinking more like an hour.'

Glancing around, Swampfire spotted an area of rocky ground. 'HighBreed, this way,' he called, racing up the hill towards the rocks.

Summoning all his strength, the HighBreed dragged himself in the direction of Swampfire's voice, kicking off the insects as he scrambled up the hillside.

When the HighBreed was out of harm's

way, Swampfire blasted a mound of rocks with a ball of flame. The stone crumbled and began to roll down the hill, causing a landslide. The tumbling boulders forced the insects back, and soon they were buried beneath a flowing river of sand.

As the ground gave way beneath his feet, the HighBreed began to fall. He slid down the hillside, his arms flailing wildly as he tried to slow himself down.

A powerful hand reached down and caught him by the arm. With a grunt, Swampfire hoisted the HighBreed back up onto the rock beside him.

'You're welcome,' smirked Swampfire, when it was obvious the alien wasn't about to thank him.

'How dare ... You filthy ...' The HighBreed yanked his arm away. 'Unhand me!'

'What is with you?' demanded Swampfire. 'Yeah, you don't like the creatures I turn into,

I get it. But c'mon, I was saving you. Cut an alien monster guy some slack once in a while.'

Angrily, Swampfire turned and stomped off across the desert. The HighBreed sat on the rock, not moving, until Swampfire returned.

With a dramatic sigh, Swampfire held out his hands, gesturing for the HighBreed to take the lead. The HighBreed alien stood up and began to walk, leaving Swampfire behind to follow in his footsteps.

'"Ten paces behind",' Swampfire mumbled, before setting off after the HighBreed.

Several hours later, as the twin suns were beginning to dip below the horizon, Swampfire was still muttering below his breath. 'The second we're off this planet I'll show him "ten paces behind",' he seethed.

Up ahead, the cool night air was giving the HighBreed new strength. He strode on, paying no attention to his companion.

'This is as good a place as any to set up camp for the night,' Swampfire announced, stopping by a rocky outcrop.

'No. We shall walk through the night.'

'No,' insisted Swampfire, mimicking the HighBreed's serious tone. 'We shall camp here for the night.'

'I would not use such an insolent tone with me, lesser creature,' growled the HighBreed, spinning to face him.

'Oh really?'

'You have not yet dealt with me at my full strength. See how the cool night air has begun to restore me?'

Swampfire nodded. 'Yeah. I noticed.'

'I shall carry on from here on my own.'

'All right, go then,' replied Swampfire.

'You have outstayed your usefulness to me,' continued the HighBreed, resuming his march across the sand.

'So have you!'

The HighBreed hadn't got very far when a piercing cry of a Dravek echoed around the desert planet. The HighBreed stopped in his tracks. He looked back at Swampfire, then off into the still darkness that lay ahead. At last he reached a decision.

'We shall camp here for the night,' he said, as if it had been his idea in the first place, and then he hurried back to join Swampfire by the rocks.

'Sure thing. Whatever you say, tough guy,' Swampfire replied.

CHAPTER FOUR

WOUNDED

Night had fallen on the desert. The flickering flames of a small campfire were the only defence against the darkness. Ben sat by the flames, enjoying the heat they gave off. The desert could get very cold at night.

'Pull up a boulder,' Ben suggested, turning to the HighBreed. 'Sit down.'

'So your infernal pit can deplete me of my strength? I think not.'

'It's a campfire. It's tradition,' explained Ben, patiently. 'You sit around it and, you know, maybe sing a song. Eat a hotdog. Talk.'

'Talk? To you?' snorted the HighBreed. 'For what conceivable purpose?'

Ben felt a little of his patience drain away, but he continued. 'My name is Ben, Ben Tennyson. What's your name?'

'I am called Reinrassig the Third, seventh son of the noble HighBreed house of Di Razza, direct descendent of the pure-blooded High Order of Rasecht, heir to the –'

'I'm gonna call you "Reiny",' said Ben, cutting him off.

'That is very disrespectful, Ben-Ben Tennyson.'

Ben shrugged and poked at the fire with a stick. The flames flared brighter. 'It's weird. Despite the fact that I honestly don't trust you any farther than Humungousaur could throw you, it's still pretty cool how we've managed to work together to survive.' He dropped the stick and warmed his hands on the fire's glow.

'I mean, we may not be the best of friends exactly, but we're not full-on mortal enemies any more either.'

'You and I will always be enemies,' the HighBreed replied.

'But we've been able to see past our differences. Probably because I know what it's like to be ... well, not a HighBreed exactly, but a whole bunch of other kinds of alien creatures kinda like you.' He held up his wrist so the HighBreed could see the Omnitrix. 'Thanks to this, I get to walk a mile in other life forms' shoes. So I can totally understand what it's like to be them, since I have been them.'

Ben sat back and nodded, proud of his little speech. For a moment the HighBreed said nothing, staring off into the distance. Then he began to speak. 'Such presumption,' he growled. 'But what else is to be expected from a genetically inferior creature?'

'I don't ... what?'

'Why would I, a HighBreed, be the slightest bit interested in befriending the revolting likes of you?'

'I'm just trying to be nice here,' Ben protested. 'Find some common ground or something.'

'You and I are more than mere enemies,' said the HighBreed, drawing himself up to his full impressive height. 'HighBreeds were the very first race in the universe. All species hence, other than pure-blooded HighBreeds, are nothing but mongrels. Hideous abominations of nature, especially humans.

'As soon as I no longer require your aid for my own protection, Ben-Ben Tennyson, I shall eradicate you. And there will be one less vermin infesting a grateful universe.'

'You can't really believe all that,' replied Ben. 'Not after everything we've been through. Not after the way I've been helping you.'

'When you weren't trying to kill me.'

Ben was too angry and frustrated to come up with a reply. Instead he shook his head and stared into the heart of the fire.

'You are tired, human,' said the HighBreed. 'I shall take the first watch.'

Ben's eyes narrowed suspiciously. Like he'd said, he didn't trust the HighBreed one bit.

'Oh no,' Bebn said, 'I'm wide awake. You get some sleep. I'll take the first watch.'

⌛ ⌛ ⌛

Neither of them had given in, but in the end it was Ben who finally fell asleep first. He lay flat on his back, snoring below his breath.

A shadow passed over him, but Ben

didn't stir. The HighBreed stared down at him, his alien eyes narrowed in disgust. Then, with a sudden jerk of his shoulder, the HighBreed raised an arm above his head.

Sensing danger, Ben flicked open his eyes. He let out a sharp gasp as he spotted the HighBreed's huge fist swinging swiftly down towards him.

SPLAAAAK!

The HighBreed's claws snapped shut

around a large bug. It looked like the ones they had fought earlier, only this one was much larger and more deadly-looking. It squirmed in the alien's grip, twisting its body until its powerful jaws were free.

The bug's mouth snapped tightly shut around the HighBreed's wrist, causing the alien to cry out in agony. The insect then forced its jaws closed further. The HighBreed howled as his hand dropped onto the sand with a plop. Pausing only to hiss at Ben, the alien bug scuttled off across the sand.

'Can you regenerate it?' asked Ben, his eyes locked on the HighBreed's severed hand.

'I am not a lowly Homo Palustris,' the HighBreed snapped, referring to the alien race from which Swampfire came.

'But it can be healed?'

'Not from such an injury as this. Not in these conditions,' replied the HighBreed, writhing in pain.

Ben's mind raced. There had to be some way to heal the HighBreed's arm. But how?

And then it hit him. Homo Palustris.

Swampfire!

Ben quickly slammed down on the Omnitrix. In a flash of green light, Ben transformed into the flame-headed plant alien. He collected the HighBreed's hand from the sand. Kneeling in front of the injured alien, Swampfire carefully pressed the hand against the stump of the wrist. Four or five tiny green pods fell from his own hand and began to burrow into the wound.

In moments the pods began to grow. As the HighBreed watched on, thin strands of plant vine wrapped tightly around the injury, reconnecting his hand to his arm.

The HighBreed held his arm up in the air. He twitched the fingers. It hurt, but at least it worked.

Swampfire changed back into Ben. 'Better?' he asked.

'Why would you help me?' the HighBreed demanded.

'Why would you help me?'

'It was in my own interest to stop that creature from harming you.'

'Yeah?' said Ben. 'Well it's in my interest to help anybody who needs it.'

The HighBreed turned away, Ben's words still ringing in his ears. Maybe, just maybe, there was a little bit more to the human race than he thought.

Ben perched on a rock and poked his stick into the fire again. The flames were dying down. He would have to go and find more sticks to burn soon.

A sudden rumble beneath him made

Ben leap up to his feet. The rock he had been sitting on trembled and shook. The HighBreed extended an arm and fired a dozen razor-sharp spikes at the stone. Almost at once, the rumbling stopped.

Ben flashed the HighBreed a grateful smile and crept back over to where he had been sitting. Cautiously, he prodded the stone with his foot. Nothing happened. Whatever had been making the rock move had now –

KRAKA-BOOOOM!

Sand suddenly erupted all around him like a huge volcanic explosion, sending rocks, stones and boulders rocketing up towards the night sky.

Ben was thrown right off balance. The wind was knocked from him as he fell and rolled backwards across the ground.

The sand and dust were carried quickly away on the breeze, revealing Ben's worst nightmare. A Dravek reared up from the sand, its wide jaws snapping and snarling. But this wasn't just any Dravek, it was the biggest Dravek they had seen so far.

And it was bearing directly down on top of Ben.

CHAPTER FIVE

CHANGES

A volley of sharp spikes embedded themselves deep in the Dravek's tough hide, distracting the creature and drawing it away from Ben. The giant worm twisted its bulky body and lunged towards the HighBreed, who had just enough time to fire off a few more shots before leaping out of the way.

The cool night air was boosting the HighBreed's strength, but his arm was still healing and he wasn't yet at full fighting fitness. As the worm-creature turned once again and raced towards him, the HighBreed had no choice but to flee for his life.

'Ben-Ben Tennyson!' he bellowed, feeling the ground beneath him quake. Still dazed from his fall, Ben looked up to see the HighBreed darting towards him, with the

Dravek right behind.

Ben was too groggy to move yet. There was no way he could get clear in time. Realising this, the HighBreed stopped, turned, then threw himself towards the Dravek's open mouth. Gripping onto the creature's jagged lips he hung there, not quite sure what to do next.

Luckily Ben was back in action. He scrambled upright and snatched a burning stick from the campfire. There was no time to go hero – he had to act and he had to act fast.

Racing back to the Dravek's mouth, Ben hurled the flaming piece of wood down its throat. The mouth snapped shut immediately, throwing the HighBreed down onto the hard-packed sand.

Thick plumes of grey smoke billowed from within the Dravek, as its toxic stomach acids caught light. It wriggled and squirmed, thrashing its powerful tail against the sand.

At last the creature opened its jaws. A jet of flame emerged, like the breath of some alien dragon, and the fire inside the Dravek went out. Ben and the HighBreed braced themselves for the battle to resume, but the worm-creature had taken enough punishment for one night. With a final snarl it burrowed its tail into the ground and sunk down out of sight.

Taking a deep breath to calm his racing heart, Ben turned to the alien at his side.

'Maybe you were right,' he admitted. 'Maybe we should walk all night.'

And walk they did. For hours they trudged across the darkened desert, watching each other's backs as they made their way towards the teleporter. Although Ben didn't say it, he was glad to have the HighBreed with him. He would never have survived on his own.

'Thanks for saving me back there,' he said. 'Again.'

The HighBreed didn't respond, choosing instead to carry on walking in silence.

'This is a huge thing,' continued Ben, excitedly. 'A sign of personal growth. Proof that underneath it all, HighBreeds aren't really so bad. That despite those terrible things you may have said before, you really do want to try to be friends with a human.'

Ben upped his pace, walking now with a spring in his step. Even though he was millions of miles from home on a desolate alien planet, he felt good. He was helping to change the HighBreed, and change him for the better.

But once again the HighBreed did not answer. He kept walking, one foot plodding steadily in front of the other, lost in his own troubling thoughts. The human was walking alongside him, not behind him.

And for some reason he couldn't understand, the HighBreed didn't mind.

It was morning when they finally reached the teleporter pod. It stood before them, scuffed by sand and bleached by the sun, but otherwise exactly like the one that had carried them to this desert world.

'There it is, come on!' yelped Ben, racing across the sand towards the machine. He stopped just a few paces on, when he realised the HighBreed wasn't following. 'Not the ten paces behind thing again?'

The HighBreed looked down, then slowly raised his head again. 'Go home, Ben-Ben Tennyson,' he said. 'I shall remain here.'

'Did you hit your head or something?' asked Ben, unable to believe what he was hearing. 'There's the teleporter. We can finally get off this sand trap of doom and back to our own lives.'

'I have spent too long with you, Ben-Ben Tennyson,' the alien said, and Ben couldn't miss the sadness in his voice. 'And have therefore myself become contaminated.'

Ben raised an eyebrow. 'Contaminated?'

'As clearly evidenced by my uncharacteristic behaviour, risking my own life to save you, a lowly human,' said the HighBreed.

'Reiny,' began Ben, softly, 'what you did was a good thing.'

'I have obviously become infected by your mongrel influence and am now unclean.'

Ben rounded on him. 'Listen, big guy, even if I believed that was true, why would you stay here?'

'In self-imposed exile. As it should be.' The HighBreed craned his neck and looked up at the two burning suns raging in the sky. 'For I can never, ever return back home. Or anywhere in fact. I could be in danger of infecting the rest of my kind. The only honourable choice is for me to remain here forever.'

'No,' said Ben.

'Because all lesser beings other than pure, unadulterated HighBreeds must be expunged from the universe.' The alien paused before adding, 'Including myself.'

'I thought I had gotten through to you,' said Ben. 'I thought you had changed.'

'This much is true. I have changed,' agreed the HighBreed. 'And now I must pay the price. I must accept this punishment. It is the only way. Goodbye Ben-Ben Tennyson.'

A thousand light years away, in a warehouse on the other side of the universe, Kevin and Gwen were poking around in the control panel of the teleporter. Everything seemed to be connected properly – the wires were in place, the switches were correctly aligned – but the thing refused to do anything. It was completely dead.

'Everything looks fine,' Kevin said, for the hundredth time in the last few hours. 'But I can't make it work.'

Gwen leaned over his shoulder, studying the machine. She was tired – they both were – but they couldn't give up.

'We've got to fix it, Kevin,' she urged. 'We have to find –'

Suddenly, a flickering blue light shimmered across the surface of the teleporter. Kevin and Gwen stepped away just as a very familiar figure stumbled through.

'Ben! You're back!' cried Gwen, rushing to meet her cousin. She threw her arms around him and they shared a warm hug.

Even Kevin looked happy to see his friend. 'Man, am I glad to see you. You gave us a big scare,' he smiled, punching Ben playfully on the arm. 'We've been trying to fix that thing for hours. We thought we'd lost you big time! Where did you go?'

'It's a long story. Just think giant sand

monsters, deadly flesh-eating bugs and a whole lot of heat.'

'Hang on, where did the HighBreed go?' Gwen asked. 'Did he get away?'

Ben looked to the floor and shook his head, sadly. 'No, I doubt it.'

Back on the deadly desert world of Turrawuste, the HighBreed sat high up on a rock examining his arm. Swampfire's vines were doing their job, and the wound was knitting together nicely. The hand had taken on a strange green tinge – the only outward sign of how his encounter with Ben-Ben Tennyson had contaminated him.

But it was the contamination inside that really mattered. The HighBreed knew it was wrong, he knew he must be sick, or mad, or both, but despite their differences he had actually found himself almost liking the strange human boy. He had felt a strange connection with the enemy.

With a shudder he stood up and stretched his tired limbs. He was hot and thirsty. He didn't have the energy to look for water in the ground. The twin suns shone brightly in the morning sky, scorching his skin and draining all of his strength. Perhaps, he decided, that was for the best.

Clambering up to the top of a rocky hill, the HighBreed took up a position atop the highest boulder. Standing up straight he stared off into the distance where he could see three huge Draveks thundering across the sand. They were too far away for him to feel the shaking of the ground, but it would not be long, he knew, until he felt the first tremors.

He looked up to the sky and nodded, satisfied that he had chosen the correct fate. He was contaminated. Filthy. Impure. And impurity had to be destroyed. All of it.

Even him.